www.mascotbooks.com

CHICKEN GIRL

For more information, please contact:
Mascot Books
620 Herndon Parkway, Suite 320
Herndon, VA 20170
info@mascotbooks.com

Library of Congress Control Number: 2018914596

CPSIA Code: PRT0219A
ISBN-13: 978-1-64307-270-8

Printed in the United States

Chicken Girl

Bonnie Tribbett Rosario   Illustrated by Cheryl Crouthamel

♡ Chicken Girl
Bonnie

Bonnie, whose hair was always tangled in curls, was a curious and happy animal-loving girl. She loved animals with fur, animals with scales, animals with prickles, and all kinds of tails. But she *ESPECIALLY* loved birds, chickens to be exact! She studied them, watched them, and wanted to own them, in fact!

To the school library each week she would go, marching to the counter and putting on quite the show! "Mrs. Whitefield," she'd say, "I know I ask you each week, but is today the day for the new chicken books I seek?" Bonnie held her breath with excitement and glee, and waited for the librarian's answer to be...

"Bonnie, dear Bonnie, you silly little girl, with the space in your teeth and the big curly curls, I don't have any new books for you today. I have the same four chicken books I had yesterday!"

Well, Bonnie was focused and didn't mind at all as the school kids watched her walk down the hall. Nose buried in her chicken books, as happy as can be, Bonnie didn't care ONE bit when she heard them say, "Gee! That girl is funny. She's a bit crazy and such. Why does she love those chickens so much?"

Her family always smiled, listening to her gab and whirl,
which is how she got the name Bonnie the Chicken Girl.

Her daddy, who loved his girl so, watched her read, study, and grow. She was a chicken expert—she'd learned everything. Perhaps she was ready for her own chickens this spring! Her daddy hatched a plan with her mommy that night, a fun family field trip with a great ending in sight!

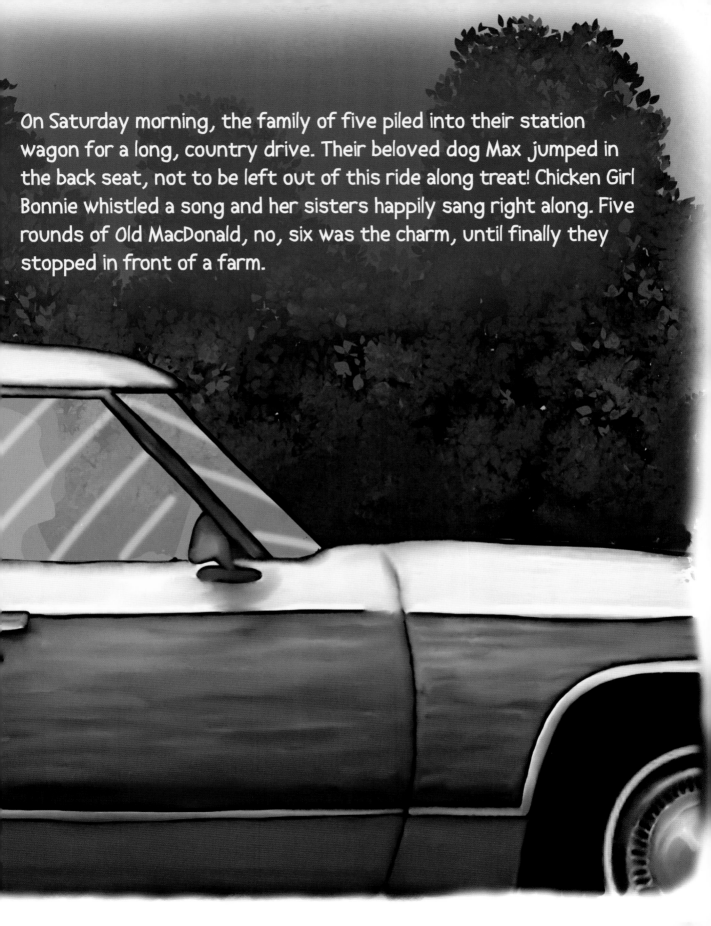

On Saturday morning, the family of five piled into their station wagon for a long, country drive. Their beloved dog Max jumped in the back seat, not to be left out of this ride along treat! Chicken Girl Bonnie whistled a song and her sisters happily sang right along. Five rounds of Old MacDonald, no, six was the charm, until finally they stopped in front of a farm.

Daddy and Mommy got out of the car, with Chicken Girl Bonnie and her sisters not far. "Why are we here? Can we go and explore?" The sisters were happy they weren't in the car anymore.

Just then the farmer's wife came out to give them a tour—baby pigs, sheep, goats, and oh, so much more. For all over the farm, looking left then right, were the animals that brought Chicken Girl such delight.

Hens over here, roosters over there, all sizes and colors, chickens everywhere! Bonnie squealed with glee, her sisters did too. Isn't that just what you'd expect them to do?

Then magical words were spoken with a nod and wink—her parents and the farmer were already in sync. "Bonnie, choose two, a rooster and hen. We know you'll choose wisely, because you've proven you can."

Perseverance paid off, her dream had come true, she began searching the farmyard for her special two. Then Chicken Girl saw them, and giggled and grinned. "That rooster over there is where I begin. And now for a hen, a special one I need, I'll take that speckled one over there by the seed!"

They went in a box in the back of their car, hugs and thank yous seemed to go far. For the farmers were pleased and knew in their hearts that Chicken Girl Bonnie was off to a great start.

The family drove home with their new feathered friends, who sat in the box wondering where their trip would end. The sisters looked over their seats with joy, wondering what to name their new girl and boy. Because chickens *NEED* names and all fell in love when they met, their new names became Romeo and Juliet!

At home, those two chickens were loved oh so much as they settled into their fancy new hutch. They had cozy new boxes to sleep in at night, with plenty of straw and green grass in sight.

Chicken Girl fed them each morning with her rain boots and pail,
and climbed in the hutch to check under Juliet's feathered tail.
She was searching for an egg, her hen's first lay, but there was
no egg laid day after day.

Until one morning Juliet laid, she finally did, which made Chicken Girl Bonnie the happiest kid!

She ran with that little brown egg in hand to show her family her new treasure so grand.

It was small in size, but that mattered not, for a hen's first egg is always small, just like the books taught.

Perfect is what Chicken Girl thought of her new friends when she visited them outside in their little grassy pen. She was proud she had learned everything they'd need, all thanks to those four chicken books she loved to read. Chicken Girl had persisted and her dream had come true, and they all lived together, one lovely chicken crew!

Now I'm sure this next part won't come as a surprise, for you see before long Chicken Girl's crew grew in size. Romeo and Juliet hatched four downy chicks, and oh how Chicken Girl loved her new brood of six!

CHICKEN GIRL'S CHICKEN FACTS

A hen's first egg is often called a fairy egg because it is so small.

It takes 21 days for an egg to hatch, either from hen or incubator.

Egg colors vary according to the type of chicken.

Chickens have a red comb on their heads and wattles on their necks.

Chickens can see in color and have eyelids that close when sleeping.

Male chickens are called roosters. Female chickens are called hens. Baby chickens are called chicks.

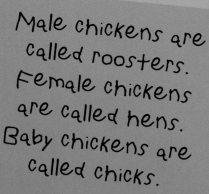

Chickens are
social birds.
A group of
chickens is called
a flock.

Chickens are
omnivores. They
eat seeds, insects,
grasses, cornmeal,
and they love
watermelon or
pumpkins as treats.

Mother hens
don't feed their
own chicks like
other birds.
Instead, she
leads them to
the food source.

Chickens need a coop or hutch for protection from predators.

Hens can lay an egg almost daily, but it also depends on their age and time of year.

Hens like to have a nesting box for egg laying.

About the Author

Bonnie Tribbett Rosario grew up in rural Pennsylvania, living in the country where she was able to raise her pet chickens. She moved to California and attended San Diego State University, where she graduated and became an elementary teacher in Imperial Beach, California. Her family moved to Hawaii for several years for her husband's Navy career, where she taught at Hickam Elementary School and Hawaii Technology Academy. Upon her husband's retirement, her family moved to and now resides in Riverside, California. She teaches kindergarten in Menifee, California. Her love of animals continues with her pet bunny rabbit who visits her classroom often, and chicks she raises each spring with her students.